PIGS

PIGS

STORY by
ROBERT MUNSCH

ART by
MICHAEL MARTCHENKO

annick press
toronto • berkeley

We acknowledge the support of the Canada Council for the Arts and the Ontario Arts Council, and the participation of the Government of Canada/la participation du gouvernement du Canada for our publishing activities.

Library and Archives Canada Cataloguing in Publication

Munsch, Robert N., 1945-, author
    Pigs / Robert Munsch ; illustrated by Michael Martchenko. – Classic Munsch edition.

Originally published: Willowdale, Ontario: Annick Press, 1985.
ISBN 978-1-77321-032-2 (hardcover).--ISBN 978-1-77321-031-5 (softcover)

    I. Martchenko, Michael, illustrator II. Title.

PS8576.U575P53 2018   jC813'.54   C2017-905732-4

Published in the U.S.A. by Annick Press (U.S.) Ltd.
Distributed in Canada by University of Toronto Press.
Distributed in the U.S.A. by Publishers Group West.

Printed in China

www.annickpress.com
www.robertmunsch.com

Also available in e-book format. Please visit www.annickpress.com/ebooks.html for more details.

To Meghan Celhoffer
Holland Centre, Ontario

Megan's father asked her to feed the pigs on her way to school. He said, "Megan, please feed the pigs, but don't open the gate. Pigs are smarter than you think. Don't open the gate."

"Right," said Megan. "I will not open the gate. Not me. No sir. No, no, no, no, no."

So Megan went to the pig pen. She looked at the pigs. The pigs looked at Megan.

Megan said, "These are the dumbest-looking animals I have ever seen. They stand there like lumps on a bump. They wouldn't do anything if I did open the gate." So Megan opened the gate just a little bit. The pigs stood there and looked at Megan. They didn't do anything.

Megan said, "These are the dumbest-looking animals I have ever seen. They stand there like lumps on a bump. They wouldn't even go out the door if the house was on fire." So Megan opened the gate a little bit more. The pigs stood there and looked at Megan. They didn't do anything.

Then Megan yelled, "HEY YOU DUMB PIGS!"

The pigs jumped up and ran right over Megan,
WAP-WAP-WAP-WAP-WAP,
and out the gate.

When Megan got up she couldn't see the pigs anywhere. She said, "Uh-oh, I am in bad trouble. Maybe pigs are not so dumb after all." Then she went to tell her father the bad news. When she got to the house Megan heard a noise coming from the kitchen. It went, "OINK, OINK, OINK."

"That doesn't sound like my mother. That doesn't sound like my father. That sounds like pigs."

She looked in the window. There was her father, sitting at the breakfast table. A pig was drinking his coffee. A pig was eating his newspaper. And a pig was peeing on his shoe. "Megan," yelled her father, "you opened the gate. Get these pigs out of here."

Megan opened the front door a little bit. The pigs stood and looked at Megan. Finally Megan opened the front door all the way and yelled,

"HEY YOU DUMB PIGS!"

The pigs jumped up and ran right over Megan,

WAP-WAP-WAP-WAP-WAP,

and out the door.

Megan ran outside, chased all the pigs into the pig pen and shut the gate. Then she looked at the pigs and said, "You are still dumb, like lumps on a bump." Then she ran off to school. Just as she was about to open the front door, she heard a sound:

"OINK, OINK, OINK."

She said, "That doesn't sound like my teacher. That doesn't sound like the principal. That sounds like pigs."

Megan looked in the principal's window. There was a pig drinking the principal's coffee. A pig was eating the principal's newspaper. And a pig was peeing on the principal's shoe. The principal yelled, "Megan, get these pigs out of here!"

Megan opened the front door of the school a little bit. The pigs didn't do anything. She opened the door a little bit more. The pigs still didn't do anything. She opened the door all the way and yelled, "HEY YOU DUMB PIGS!" The pigs jumped up and ran right over Megan, WAP-WAP-WAP-WAP-WAP, and out the door.

Megan went into the school. She sat down at her desk and said, "That's that! I finally got rid of all the pigs." Then she heard a noise: "OINK, OINK, OINK."

Megan opened her desk, and there was a new baby pig. The teacher said, "Megan! Get that dumb pig out of here!"

Megan said, "Dumb? Who ever said pigs were dumb? Pigs are smart. I am going to keep it for a pet."

At the end of the day the school bus finally came. Megan walked up to the door, then heard something say,
"OINK, OINK, OINK."

Megan said, "That doesn't sound like the bus driver. That sounds like a pig." She climbed up the stairs and looked in the bus. There was a pig driving the bus, pigs eating the seats, and pigs lying in the aisle.

A pig shut the door and drove the
bus down the road.

It drove the bus all the way to
Megan's farm, through the
barnyard, and right into
the pig pen.

Megan got out of the bus, walked across the barnyard, and marched into the kitchen. She said, "The pigs are all back in the pig pen. They came back by themselves. Pigs are smarter than you think."

And Megan never let out any more animals.

At least, not any more PIGS.

Even More Classic Munsch:

The Dark
Mud Puddle
The Paper Bag Princess
The Boy in the Drawer
Jonathan Cleaned Up, Then He Heard a Sound
Millicent and the Wind
Mortimer
The Fire Station
Angela's Airplane
David's Father
Thomas' Snowsuit
50 Below Zero
I Have to Go!
Moira's Birthday
A Promise is a Promise
Something Good
Show and Tell
Purple, Green and Yellow
Wait and See
Where is Gah-Ning?
From Far Away
Stephanie's Ponytail
Munschworks: The First Munsch Collection
Munschworks 2: The Second Munsch Treasury
Munschworks 3: The Third Munsch Treasury
Munschworks 4: The Fourth Munsch Treasury
The Munschworks Grand Treasury
Munsch Mini-Treasury One
Munsch Mini-Treasury Two
Munsch Mini-Treasury Three

For information on these titles please visit www.annickpress.com
Many Munsch titles are available in French and/or Spanish, as well as in
board book and e-book editions. Please contact your favorite supplier.